Robin Hood

羅賓漢

Retold by Silvana Sardi
Illustrated by Paola Chartroux

The Commercial Press

Contents 目錄

故事錄音開始和結束的標記
start ▶ **stop** ■

MAIN CHARACTERS

ROBIN HOOD

MARIAN

LITTLE JOHN

WILL SCARLETT

THE SHERIFF OF NOTTINGHAM

KING RICHARD THE LION HEART

Reading

1 **How much do you already know about Robin Hood?**
Decide if the following statements are true (T) or false (F).

	T	F
Robin Hood lived in Sherwood Forest.	✓	☐
1 The Sheriff of Nottingham was Robin's friend.	☐	☐
2 Robin lived with his mother and father in the forest.	☐	☐
3 King Henry wasn't kind to his people.	☐	☐
4 Robin only stole from the rich.	☐	☐
5 Robin and his Merry Men used guns.	☐	☐
6 The ordinary people of Nottingham hated Robin Hood.	☐	☐
7 Robin was in love with Marian.	☐	☐

2a Match the words that mean the same.

z harm		**z** hurt
1 ☐ help		**a** criminal
2 ☐ outlaw		**b** rob
3 ☐ angry		**c** wealthy
4 ☐ rich		**d** aid
5 ☐ steal		**e** annoyed

2b Complete the following sentences with a word from the first column.

Robin Hood didn't _steal_ from the poor.

1 The Sheriff got _____ when he couldn't catch Robin Hood.

2 Robin Hood tried to _____ the poor.

3 The _____ people of Nottingham were afraid of being robbed.

4 The Sheriff of Nottingham called Robin an _____.

Vocabulary

3 **Read the clues and complete the crossword.**

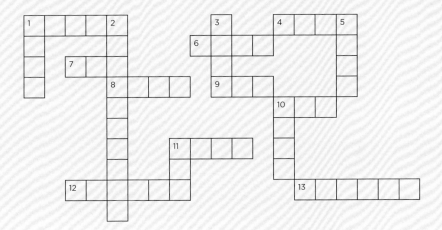

ACROSS
1 The hero of the story.
4 right, fair or a moment ago.
6 Part of a tree.
7 to allow, permit.
8 Robin and his men made a good one.
9 to steal.
10 ... name is Robin.
11 To give a hand, aid.
12 Robin was this for his men.
13 A person who uses a bow and arrow.

DOWN
1 The kind of person Robin stole from.
2 The Sheriff of...
3 An animal of the forest.
5 A big plant in the forest.
10 Robin used this to cover his head.
11 ... name is Marian.

Chapter 1

Robin Hood and Will Scarlett

▶2 It was a warm sunny day in Sherwood Forest. Robin Hood was enjoying the peace and quiet under the shade of a big oak tree. He loved this forest where he lived with his band of Merry Men. They were his family now, since the Sheriff of Nottingham had killed his parents and taken all his land.

'Probably the Sheriff is looking for me now,' thought Robin.

The Sheriff called him 'The Outlaw[1] Robin Hood' because Robin and his men helped the poor people of Nottingham: they stole from the rich to give to the poor.

King Henry wanted to become richer and richer and invented a new tax every day, so many people did not have enough money to live. Robin Hood and his men tried to help these people, so the poor loved them but the rich hated them.

Robin and his band of men were all good archers[2]. This was important for hunting and

1. **outlaw:** 亡命之徒 ▶SYN◀ criminal
2. **archers:** 弓箭手

defending themselves against the Sheriff's soldiers. However they never harmed[1] their rich victims. Instead they outwitted[2] them.

Suddenly Robin heard a noise. He jumped up quickly and hid behind the tree. Nearby, a young man was about to shoot a deer with his bow and arrow[3].

'Put down your arrow at once!' Robin said.

'Who do you think you are to give me such orders?' asked the stranger.

Robin was about to get angry, when he noticed something familiar about the boy, so he said:

'I am Robin Hood. May I have the pleasure of knowing your name?'

The young man was very surprised and, in a trembling[4] voice, he asked:

'Robin, do you really not recognise your cousin? Has the war changed me so much?'

'Do you mean you are William Gamwell? William Gamwell, better known as Will Scarlett because of the colour of your hair?'

In reply, William pushed back his hood to show

1. **harmed:** 傷害 ▶SYN◀ to hurt
2. **outwitted:** 以機智取勝
3. **bow and arrow:** 弓箭
4. **trembling:** 顫抖 ▶SYN◀ shaky

his head of curly red hair. The two young men laughed and cried at the same time; they were so happy to see each other!

However, this happy moment ended when Will asked Robin about his family.

'I'm sorry Will, but the King forced[1] your family to leave Gamwell Hall and took all your land. They are now living in a smaller house in Barnsdale with Maude and Marian.'

'But are they all well?' asked Will.

'Yes, my dear cousin,' Robin answered. 'They are all well, even if less rich. But it is more important that they still have each other to love.'

'You are right Robin,' agreed Will, 'but my father made his fortune as an honest man. This is all so unfair[2]!'

'I know,' said Robin. 'Why don't you join me and my band of Merry Men? Together we can fight against the King and his friends!'

'I would be honoured!' exclaimed Will.

'In that case you must meet my men,' said Robin, and he blew on his horn[3]. In a few seconds,

1. **forced:** 威逼 ▶SYN◀ to oblige
2. **unfair:** 不公平 ▶PET◀ ▶SYN◀ unjust, wrong
3. **horn:** 號角

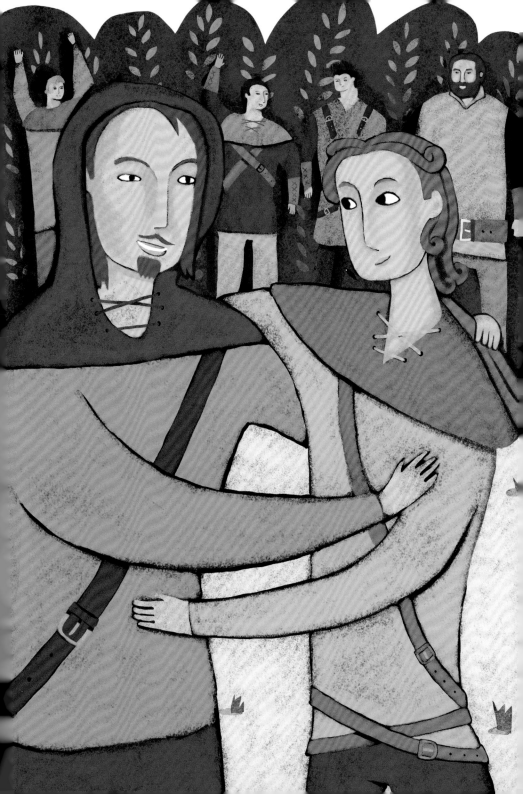

about a hundred men appeared, all dressed in green like Robin.

That evening, at their hideout[1] in the forest, they had a big dinner to celebrate Will's return. During the meal, Will said he wanted to go to Barnsdale the next day to see his family again. Robin and two of his men, Much and Little John, decided to go with him.

Early next morning, they happily set out[2] on foot for Barnsdale. Will Scarlett was excited about seeing his family again and the girl he loved: Maude... his sweet, beautiful Maude. Will was lost in his dreams and only realised that he had spoken his thoughts aloud[3], when Robin and Much laughed and said: 'Maude, Maude, my sweet beautiful Maude!' William became as red as his curly hair.

'You shouldn't laugh, Robin,' he said. 'While you were sleeping last night, I heard you say the name of your loved one, Marian.'

Now it was Robin's turn to feel embarrassed and everyone laughed again.

1. hideout: 巢穴
2. set out: 出發 ▶PET◀ ▶SYN◀ to leave
3. aloud: 大聲地 ▶PET◀

On the road to Barnsdale, they decided to stop at an inn[1] for the night. Robin pulled his hood down over his face in case the Sheriff's men were in town. They sat at a table drinking and talking. Will Scarlett looked up as two men came into the inn. One of the men looked at Will intensely, then quickly left the room. Will was excited about seeing his family again, and said nothing about the stranger[2] to his friends.

The following morning, Much and Little John decided to return to Sherwood Forest. Robin and Will continued their journey.

When they arrived at the house, Robin entered first, to prepare Will's parents: he was afraid the shock would be too much for them.

At last Will embraced[3] his mother and father again and his two sisters, and everyone cried for joy.

Maude and Marian were not there. They were out walking, so the two young men went to look for them. They soon saw the girls in the garden. Will was suddenly[4] afraid.

1. **inn:** 小旅館
2. **stranger:** 陌生人 ▶PET◀
3. **embraced:** 擁抱
4. **suddenly:** 突然 ▶PET◀ ▶KET◀ ▶SYN◀ unexpectedly

'And if Maude doesn't like me anymore, what shall I do Robin?' he asked sadly.

'Are you mad Will Scarlett? You are talking about Maude, who loves you so much. How can you doubt[1] her love?' asked Robin.

Will had no time to answer, because at that moment the girls turned round and saw the two young men. They ran to each other, shouting for joy.

'Will, you are safe at last!' exclaimed Maude.

'Yes my beautiful Maude,' replied Will, kissing her tenderly. 'I will never leave you again. Please say you will marry me my dear Maude and we can be together forever!'

'Yes, of course my love. I will be the happiest woman in England!' she exclaimed.

Meanwhile Robin and Marian stood together hand in hand, watching the scene. They too were in love, but Robin did not want his beautiful Marian to live like an outlaw in the forest.

Moreover, Marian was also worried about her brother Allan. He was away fighting in the war and nobody knew exactly where he was.

1. doubt: 懷疑

'Marian, I will bring you back your brother! Then, when I have my home and land again, we too will marry,' promised Robin.

'Bring me back my brother, but do not worry about the house or land. I will be happy to live anywhere with you,' replied Marian.

The young couple kissed, then followed Maude and Will who were running home to tell everyone about their wedding[1] plans.

The ceremony was arranged[2] for the following day and everyone prepared for the happy event.

Next morning, however, when they went to call Will, they could find him nowhere.

1. **wedding:** 婚禮 ▶PET◀ ▶SYN◀ marriage
2. **arranged:** 安排 ▶PET◀ ▶SYN◀ to organise

After-reading Activities

Reading

1 Each of the following sentences refers to one of the characters in chapter 1. Write the name of the character in the space provided.

He loved this forest where he lived with his band of Merry Men .....*Robin Hood*.....

1 He had killed Robin's parents and taken all his land.................................

2 He wanted to become richer and richer and invented a new tax every day........................

3 He pushed back his hood to show his head of curly red hair.................................

4 He pulled his hood down over his face.................................

5 'I will be the happiest woman in England'
....

6 She was also worried about her brother Allan.................................

2 Complete the sentences with the verbs in the correct tense.

| be   not marry   have (2)   not be   not catch |
| meet   not see   blow   sit |

Robin *has been* an outlaw since his parents died.

1 At the moment Robin.............. under a tree in the forest.

2 The Sheriff .... Robin yet.

3 Two days ago Robin .... his cousin in the forest.

4 Last night they......................... a big dinner at their hideout.

5 Now Will's parents .... as rich as before.

6 Will .... Maude for a long time and he can't wait to get home.

7 Robin .... Marian until he .... his land once more.

8 Robin's Men always come when he .... on his horn.

Grammar

3 **Put the words in the correct order to make questions, then discuss the answers with a partner.**

Robin / live / with/ does/ who ?

Who does Robin live with?

1 Will Scarlett / colour / got / hair/ of / has / what ?
2 rich / why / from / Robin / steal / the / does ?
3 parents / Sheriff of Nottingham / did / whose / kill / the ?
4 is / get / Maude / to / when / married / going ?
5 brother / is / in / whose / the / fighting / away / war ?
6 call / men / does / his / Robin / how ?
7 does / hunt / archer / to / what / an / use / deer ?
8 many / there / in / men / Robin's / how / are / band ?
9 say / sleeping / name / Robin / did / while/ was / whose / he ?
10 the / happened / wedding / of / day/ what / the / on ?

Before-reading Activity

PET-Speaking

4 **At the end of chapter 1 nobody can find Will Scarlett. Work in pairs.**
Discuss the following questions:

1 What do you think has happened to Will ?
2 Where could he be ?
3 Are there any suspicious characters in chapter 1 who could be involved ?
4 Did anything strange happen in chapter 1 before Will disappeared?
5 What's the best way to find him?

Once you have discussed your ideas with your partner, tell the rest of the class.

Chapter 2

The Sheriff of Nottingham's wicked plans

▶ 3   The day after poor Will disappeared, there was a secret meeting between the Sheriff of Nottingham and Sir Tristan Goldsborough at Nottingham Castle.

Sir Tristan was a very old, ugly[1] man, but he was also one of the richest men in England. He wished to marry Christabel, the Sheriff of Nottingham's beautiful daughter. The Sheriff was an ambitious, greedy[2] man and did not care about his daughter's happiness. He cared only about Sir Tristan's money.

'My dear Sir Tristan,' began the Sheriff, 'as you know, my daughter is one of the most beautiful girls in England, so we must agree on a sum[3] that respects her beauty and dignity.'

'Sir, you can be certain that I will love your daughter with all my heart,' replied Sir Tristan.

'I am not interested in these silly romantic notions[4],' said the Sheriff arrogantly. 'Let's talk about money instead!'

1. **ugly:** 醜陋的 ▶PET◀ ▶SYN◀ grotesque, unattractive
2. **greedy:** 貪婪的 ▶SYN◀ avid
3. **sum:** 金額 ▶PET◀
4. **notions:** 想法 ▶SYN◀ idea

The old man sat down slowly in an armchair, while the Sheriff waited impatiently.

'Well?' asked the Sheriff. 'May I have an answer or must I wait another hour?'

'You have no respect for your elders[1]!' said Sir Tristan angrily.

'And you have little respect for my daughter's youth[2]!' answered the Sheriff. 'I ask you for the last time, how much will you give me in exchange for my daughter's hand?'

'I offer you one hundred pieces of gold.'

'What?' exploded the Sheriff. 'You are mad Sir, and you offend me with this ridiculous sum. Please leave immediately!'

Sir Tristan was not stupid. At his age, it would be very difficult to find another bride[3] as pretty and young as Christabel, so finally he said:

'Alright you win, Sheriff of Nottingham. I will give you half of my fortune in exchange for your daughter's hand.'

The Sheriff was delighted[4] with this proposal. He was just about to offer Sir Tristan something

1. **elders:** 長輩
2. **youth:** 青春 ▶PET◀
3. **bride:** 新娘 ▶PET◀
4. **delighted:** 快樂的 ▶PET◀ ▶SYN◀ very pleased

to drink, when a messenger from the King arrived.

'What news do you bring?' the Sheriff asked the messenger.

'We have caught the soldier who ran away from his regiment[1],' replied the messenger.

'And why did this dirty traitor[2] desert his King?'

'We do not know Sir, but he killed his Captain in order to escape.'

'Then I hope that the King wishes to punish him well,' said the Sheriff.

'Yes indeed, the prisoner must be hanged without mercy,' said the soldier.

'Well, put the prisoner in the castle dungeons[3] and tomorrow he will be hanged!' ordered the Sheriff.

The messenger ran off to give these orders, and Sir Tristan and the Sheriff drank together.

The Sheriff of Nottingham was very pleased with his agreement with Sir Tristan. He would soon become a very rich man which would also give him more power.

He had already forgotten about the poor soldier to be hanged the next day.

---

1. regiment: 軍團
2. traitor: 叛徒 ▶SYN◀ disloyal person
3. dungeons: 地牢

Outside in the castle courtyard[1], a young red-haired boy walked sadly between two soldiers as they led him to his prison. Will Scarlett had been caught!

Meanwhile, Robin was searching for Will everywhere. Then, near Barnsdale, he met Much.

'Robin, I am so glad to see you. I have news about poor Will Scarlett,' began Much.

'Why do you say poor?' asked Robin in fear. 'What has happened to him?'

'The King's soldiers have captured him and now he is in prison in Nottingham Castle.'

'Oh no!' exclaimed Robin. 'There is no time to waste[2] Much. Let's go to our men in the forest and make a plan to free[3] Will.'

Robin Hood told his men to wait in the forest near Nottingham Castle. Then he sent Much into town to find out more about Will.

While waiting for Much to come back, he saw an elegant knight[4] riding towards him.

'This is my chance to steal from a rich knight,' thought Robin. He needed money to buy bows and

1. courtyard: 中庭
2. to waste: 浪費 ▶PET◀
3. to free: 使自由 ▶SYN◀ to liberate
4. knight: 騎士 ▶SYN◀ horseman, nobleman

arrows for his men to attack Nottingham Castle.

'Good Day to you, my fine Lord,' said Robin to the traveller. 'What brings you to Sherwood Forest?'

'Good Day to you too stranger,' replied the knight. 'May I ask if you are one of Robin Hood's Merry Men?' he continued with a smile.

Robin was very surprised by the knight's words. 'Either this stranger is very brave[1] or very stupid,' he thought.

'My noble friend,' continued Robin, 'we are not all outlaws in this forest. You must be one of the Sheriff of Nottingham's friends for sure.'

'I am as much his friend as you are, Robin Hood!' exclaimed the stranger. 'I am Allan Clare, I recognised you as soon as I saw you!'

'Allan Clare? Marian's brother?' Robin asked in surprise[2].

'Exactly my dear Robin Hood. I have come back from the war where I was lucky and made a small fortune. Now I am going to see the Sheriff of Nottingham. He made an agreement[3] with me many years ago and now he must keep his promise.'

---

1. **brave:** 勇敢的 ▶PET◀ ▶SYN◀ ▶KET◀ courageous
2. **in surprise:** 驚訝地 ▶SYN◀ astonished
3. **agreement:** 協議 ▶SYN◀ contract

'I am happy for your good fortune, dear Allan, but I would not trust[1] the Sheriff of Nottingham to keep his promise,' said Robin.

'But you do not understand Robin,' continued Allan Clare. 'Before the war, I was already in love with the Sheriff's beautiful daughter Christabel. At that time the Sheriff said I was too poor to marry his daughter. Now I am richer than the Sheriff, so I am sure that he will be happy to let[2] me marry Christabel!' said Allan triumphantly.

'Then we must go to Nottingham Castle together my friend,' said Robin. 'I, to free Will Scarlett, and you to free Christabel from her greedy father!'

'Do you mean Will from Gamwell?' asked Allan.

'Yes. While William was away at war, his captain was very cruel. One day, they had an argument[3] and Will pushed the captain. The man fell, hit his head and died instantly.'

'Oh no,' said Allan. 'And what did Will do then?'

'He ran away and came back to England. Now they have arrested him and he is in the dungeons of Nottingham Castle.'

---

1. **trust:** 相信 ▶PET◀ ▶SYN◀ to have faith in
2. **to let:** 允許 ▶PET◀ ▶KET◀ ▶SYN◀ to permit
3. **argument:** 爭執 ▶SYN◀ disagreement

Just then, Much arrived with even worse news.

'Robin' said Much, 'we must act quickly. They plan to hang Will Scarlett tomorrow at dawn[1].'

'But why so soon?' asked Robin horrified[2].

'Because the Sheriff must organise his daughter's wedding, which will take place[3] at the end of this week,' Much explained.

This time Allan was horrified. 'What!' he shouted 'Who is she going to marry?'

'The richest man in England, Sir Tristan Goldsborough,' said Much.

Allan was so angry that he punched[4] the nearest tree and nearly broke his hand.

'Come my friend,' said Robin to Allan. 'We must go to the castle immediately to save Will.'

'And to save my poor Christabel from the hands of that ugly monster!' added Allan angrily.

So the three men set off on horseback for Nottingham Castle.

When they reached the castle, Allan went directly to speak to the Sheriff. Robin hid among the trees to decide what to do next.

---

1. dawn: 黎明 ▶SYN◀ sunrise
2. horrified: 驚恐的 ▶SYN◀ alarmed
3. take place: 發生 ▶PET◀ ▶SYN◀ to happen
4. punched: 用拳重擊 ▶SYN◀ to hit hard

After-reading Activities

Reading

1 **Unscramble the adjectives in the box, then complete the sentences about the characters.**

~~Ido~~	eatubufli	yugl	crih	deyger
	treypt	gunyo	egltena	

Sir Tristan was an o l d man.

1 The Sheriff of Nottingham was a _ _ _ _ _ _ man and wanted as much money as he could get.

2 Christabel was the Sheriff of Nottingham's_ _ _ _ _ _ _ _ _ daughter.

3 Sir Tristan was very _ _ _ _.

4 Allan Clare had made his fortune and came home a _ _ _ _ man.

5 Christabel would make a _ _ _ _ _ _ bride.

6 Allan Clare was a very _ _ _ _ _ _ _ Knight.

7 Christabel was a _ _ _ _ _ woman with hopes and dreams for the future.

Grammar

2 **Complete the following table with the comparative and superlative forms of the adjectives used in the sentences above.**

Adjective	Comparative	Superlative
old	older	the oldest
1		
2		
3		
4		
5		
6		
7		

Grammar

3 **Transform the following adjectives into adverbs. They are all mentioned in chapter 2.**

arrogant   *arrogantly*
1 impatient   ....
2 immediate   ....
3 good   ....
4 sad   ....
5 triumphant   ....
6 instant   ....
7 quick   ....
8 angry   ....

PET-Grammar

4 **Here are some sentences about chapter 2. Complete the second sentence so that it means the same as the first. Use no more than three words.**

The day after there was a secret meeting between the Sheriff of Nottingham and Sir Tristan Goldsborough.
The day after the Sheriff of Nottingham and Sir Tristan Goldsborough *met secretly*.

1 Sir Tristan was the richest man in England at that time.
There was .... rich as Sir Tristan in England at that time.

2 He was too old to marry Christabel.
He wasn't .... to marry Christabel.

3 'Please leave immediately!' said the Sheriff to Sir Tristan.
The Sheriff told Sir Tristan ....

4 Will Scarlett had been caught.
Some soldiers .... Will Scarlett prisoner.

5 'I would not trust the Sheriff,' said Robin.
Robin told Allan that the Sheriff was .... trusted.

Chapter 3

Robin and the Sheriff of Nottingham

▶ 4   An old monk[1] left the castle dungeons sadly. They were going to hang this poor boy next morning, and there was nothing he could do to stop them. He knew in his heart that Will Scarlett was not bad. Will was telling the truth when he said that the captain's death had been an accident.

As he was walking home, a man dressed in green stopped him.

'If you are looking for money, then I am the wrong person,' said the monk.

'Do not worry, I do not want to harm you. I wish only to know if you have any news of the prisoner in Nottingham Castle,' explained Robin Hood kindly.

'Ah yes, there will be a public hanging in Nottingham market square at dawn tomorrow,' said the old monk sadly.

'I have promised the poor boy that I will be there at the gallows[2] with him tomorrow, to give him what little comfort I can,' he continued.

---

1. **monk:** 僧侶
2. **gallows:** 絞刑架

As the monk was speaking, Robin started to think of a plan to save his cousin.

Meanwhile, Allan was speaking to the Sheriff of Nottingham. The Sheriff was not happy that the young man still wanted to marry his daughter.

'When I left for the war, we agreed that I could marry your daughter if I became a rich man Sir,' began Allan.

'Yes indeed,' interrupted the Sheriff 'and from what I can see,' he said, looking at Allan's clothes dirty[1] from travelling, 'you are still a poor man!'

'No!' shouted Allan. 'You are wrong Sir. I have made my fortune and I am now a rich man.'

'How rich?' asked the Sheriff immediately, his little black eyes lighting up[2] at the thought of an even bigger offer than Sir Tristan's.

'Rich enough to make your daughter happy,' replied Allan.

The Sheriff needed time to discover just how rich Allan was, so he said:

'I'm afraid that I must finish our conversation here for the moment. Tomorrow I must attend

---

1. **dirty:** 骯髒的 ▶PET◀ ▶KET◀
2. **lighting up:** 發光 ▶SYN◀ to become bright

a boring hanging. I will call you soon and we can talk more,' and with these words he almost pushed Allan out of the door.

The Sheriff soon discovered that Allan was now a rich man, but Sir Tristan was still richer. He had no intention of letting Allan ruin his plans, so he called three of his cruellest servants and said:

'Follow the young man who has just left the castle and make sure[1] he never sees the light of day again!'

At the same time in the forest, Robin was having a meeting with his men. They were talking about how to attack the castle the following day. For a second, Robin thought of his friend Allan. Had he convinced the Sheriff to keep his promise? Just then[2], Much asked him another question, and Robin forgot about his friend and concentrated on their plans to save Will.

Meanwhile, Allan was walking through the forest looking for Robin and his men. He was thinking about the Sheriff and Christabel and did not realise that he was in danger.

---

1. **make sure:** 確認 ▶PET◀ ▶SYN◀ to be certain
2. **just then:** 就在此時 ▶SYN◀ at that moment

Suddenly something hard hit him on the back of his head, and Allan fell to the ground. He tried to stand up, but again they hit him, and this time he fainted[1].

The Sheriff's servants were about to strike[2] again, when luckily, Little John appeared behind them.

His real name was John Little, but everyone called him 'Little John' as a joke[3], because he was the strongest and tallest man in the country.

Little John lifted[4] all three men at once, banged their heads together, then dropped them unconscious on the ground.

Then, he lifted Allan carefully and carried him back to the camp.

'Robin,' said Little John, 'look who I found while hunting a deer[5] for tonight's dinner!'

'Allan!' exclaimed Robin, as Little John gently put Allan on the ground.

When he heard that the Sheriff's men had tried to kill his friend, Robin was even more determined to free Will and save Christabel from her father's wicked plans.

---

1. **fainted:** 暈倒 ▶SYN◀ to lose consciousness
2. **to strike:** 打；襲擊 PET ▶SYN◀ to hit, bang
3. **as a joke:** 開玩笑地 ▶SYN◀ for fun
4. **lifted:** 提起 ▶PET◀ ▶SYN◀ to raise, lift up
5. **deer:** 鹿

While they were caring for Allan at Robin Hood's camp, Will Scarlett sat crying in the dark dungeons of Nottingham Castle. 'Please, someone help me! Tomorrow they will hang me and I will never see my sweet Maude again!' he cried. He could not sleep and lay in the darkness hoping that the light of dawn would never come.

At sunrise, however, Will heard the guards opening the door of his cell. They took him to Nottingham market square. The Sheriff was there with a crowd[1] to see the hanging.

Will looked for a familiar face but saw nobody. Then he looked at the Sheriff and said:

'I am a soldier. You cannot hang me like a common thief[2]. Give me a sword[3] and I will fight your men till I die.'

'Be quiet!' shouted the Sheriff. 'You are a murderer, you deserve[4] no pity! You will die on the gallows and I hope that outlaw Robin Hood will soon join you!'

The old monk, as promised, was standing nearby.

Just as the Sheriff ordered the hangman to proceed, the monk spoke.

1. **crowd:** 群眾 ▶PET◀ ▶KET◀
2. **thief:** 竊賊 ▶PET◀
3. **sword:** 劍
4. **deserve:** 應得 ▶PET◀ ▶SYN◀ to merit

'Please my Lord, may I give this young boy a final blessing[1]?' asked the monk.

The Sheriff was really irritated, but in front of this crowd, he could not say no. He ordered his soldiers to step back a little, and said impatiently:

'Be quick, as I have more important business to do today.'

The monk whispered[2] in the boy's ear: 'Do not be afraid Will, I am here to save you!'

Will recognised the familiar voice of his cousin Robin Hood and almost jumped for joy.

'I am going to cut your hands free[3] Will,' continued Robin, 'then you must take the sword hidden under my clothes and we will attack the soldiers.'

Everyone stood in silence. Then suddenly, Will's hands were free and he was holding a sword. Robin pulled off his disguise[4], and stood ready to fight the soldiers. They were so surprised that they didn't move.

'My Lord,' said Robin to the Sheriff, 'William Scarlett is one of my men and I have come to take him

---

1. final blessing: 最後的祝福
2. whispered: 低聲地說 ▶SYN◀ to speak softly
3. to cut free: 解救出來 ▶SYN◀ to unloosen, release
4. disguise: 喬裝

home. In exchange, you can find the three rogues[1] you sent to kill Allan Clare in my forest.'

The Sheriff shouted in anger: 'Five hundred pieces of gold for the person who catches this outlaw Robin Hood!'

Before anyone could move, Robin gave three blasts[2] of his horn. Suddenly about a hundred of his men surrounded the market square.

At this sight, the cowardly[3] Sheriff rode as fast as he could back to Nottingham Castle. The villagers and soldiers quickly followed him on foot.

Robin and his men laughed and shouted at the Sheriff and his soldiers. They chased[4] them through the town back to Nottingham Castle. Then, with Will Scarlett sitting on Little John's shoulders like a trophy, they went back to Sherwood Forest and celebrated all night. ▪

1. **rogues:** 流氓 ▶SYN◀ rascals
2. **blasts:** 吹奏 ▶SYN◀ blow
3. **cowardly:** 懦弱的
4. **chased:** 追捕 ▶SYN◀ to pursue, run after

After-reading Activities

Reading

1 Choose the correct answer – A, B or C.

Who went to visit Will Scarlett in the castle dungeons?

A ☐ Robin

B ☑ An old monk

C ☐ Allan Clare

1 When were they going to hang Will Scarlett?

A ☐ at sunrise

B ☐ at sunset

C ☐ in the afternoon

2 Who did the Sheriff of Nottingham want his daughter to marry?

A ☐ Allan Clare

B ☐ Sir Tristan Goldsborough

C ☐ Robin Hood

3 What happened to Allan Clare in the forest?

A ☐ he fell and hit his head

B ☐ he was hit on the head and fainted

C ☐ he fainted because he was hungry

4 Who rescued Allan Clare?

A ☐ Big John

B ☐ John Big

C ☐ Little John

5 Where did they take Will Scarlett to be hanged?

A ☐ to Sherwood Forest.

B ☐ to Nottingham market square

C ☐ to the Castle courtyard

6 What did the soldiers do when Robin Hood pulled off his disguise?

A ☐ They ran back to Nottingham Castle immediately

B ☐ They pulled out their swords and began to fight.

C ☐ They didn't move.

Vocabulary

2 Complete the sentences with one of the words from the box.

dungeons crowd money sword gallows thief deer

There was a big _crowd_ in the market square.

1 The old monk thought Robin wanted ....
2 Little John went into the forest to hunt ....
3 The Sheriff thought that Will Scarlett was a common ....
4 Will Scarlett sat crying in the dark .... of Nottingham Castle.
5 The .... were set up in Nottingham market square.
6 Will Scarlett held the .... in his hand, ready to fight the soldiers.

Before-reading Activity

PET-Listening

3 Listen to the extract from chapter 4. Decide if the following sentences are correct (A) or incorrect (B).

	A	B
The Sheriff of Nottingham felt happy the following day.	☐	☑
1 He was afraid the villagers wouldn't like him anymore.	☐	☐
2 The Sheriff didn't like how his soldiers had reacted to Robin Hood.	☐	☐
3 The soldiers didn't think that it was their fault.	☐	☐
4 The Sheriff ordered his men to take a train into town.	☐	☐
5 The people had to pay more tax.	☐	☐
6 The money would be used to protect the outlaws.	☐	☐
7 The people could go and pay the tax in the prison.	☐	☐

Chapter 4

Love and Weddings

▶ 5　The Sheriff of Nottingham woke up next morning in a terrible mood. After yesterday's disaster, the villagers and his soldiers might not be afraid of him anymore. This would make life very difficult for him. He decided to act quickly, and called his soldiers.

'You cowards[1]!' he shouted. 'You should all hang for what you did yesterday. You ran away from those thieves. Now your King and your country are in great danger. Those wicked outlaws will think that nobody can stop them. You were armed[2] and should have fought like real soldiers!'

He was very convincing. The soldiers really believed that it was all their fault[3], and felt very ashamed[4].

The Sheriff was pleased to see their sad faces and ordered them to do many hours of hard training.

Then he told his soldiers to go into town.

'Tell the people they must pay more tax,' said the Sheriff.

1. cowards: 懦夫
2. armed: 有武器的 ▶SYN◀ with weapons
3. fault: 過失 ▶PET◀
4. felt ashamed: 感到羞恥 ▶SYN◀ to feel guilty, remorse

'We need more money to protect them from the outlaws in the area. If they do not pay, they will go to prison!'

Now that all his military problems were solved, the Sheriff of Nottingham could concentrate on his personal affairs.

He thought about Robin Hood's words: 'the three rogues sent to kill Allan Clare…'

'Is Allan Clare dead or not?' he wondered. He was not interested in his own men's fate[1].

If Allan were dead, his problems would be over[2] and Sir Tristan could marry Christabel. The Sheriff had high ambitions for his daughter. Sir Tristan was old and would probably die soon after the wedding. Christabel would become a rich widow[3] and would be free to marry someone of the Court, maybe even a member of the Royal Family.

Again the Sheriff thought of Robin Hood's words 'sent to kill Allan Clare…'

'Allan Clare must be dead!' he thought.

His small, black eyes shone, and his thin lips formed into a wicked smile.

---

1. **fate:** 命運 ▶SYN◀ destiny
2. **to be over:** 完結 ▶PET◀ ▶SYN◀ to be finished
3. **widow:** 寡婦

In another part of the castle, Sir Tristan was also thinking about the wedding.

He was worried about having the ceremony in the Castle Chapel[1]. He did not trust the Sheriff of Nottingham, and wanted the wedding in Linton Abbey. He would feel safer there with more people around him.

Therefore he decided to go and speak to the Sheriff.

After listening to the old man, the Sheriff said:

'But my dear Sir Tristan, I suggested the Castle Chapel for your own safety[2].'

'What do you mean?' asked Sir Tristan.

'Well, we both know that Christabel is not happy about this wedding, so maybe Robin Hood and his band of murderers might try and save her.'

'I am sure that my servants will protect me,' replied the old man.

'Well, it is your decision. Now,' continued the Sheriff, 'when are you going to give me my money?'

'Do not worry Sir, your precious gold is in a chest[3] which I will bring to you the day of the wedding.'

'Well, I am glad all is settled[4],' said the Sheriff,

1. **chapel:** 小教堂
2. **safety:** 安全 ▶SYN◀ security
3. **chest:** 寶箱
4. **settled:** 解決 ▶SYN◀ to decide, conclude

opening the door to indicate their conversation was over.

At Barnsdale Hall, everybody thought Will was dead. The family, Maude and Marian were sadly sitting together talking about Will. Suddenly, Marian heard the sound of Robin's horn in the distance. They all ran out to the courtyard. There, arriving on horseback was Robin, Allan Clare and Will!

Will rushed[1] to kiss Maude. Marian didn't know who to kiss first, her brother Allan or Robin.

She was so happy to see her brother again, and so proud[2] of Robin that she said:

'Look everyone, my love, my hero Robin Hood! Please Allan, now that you are home, give us your blessing[3] so that we may get married!'

'Of course, my sister, you have my blessing. I could not think of a better man for you!'

'But I have no home for you Marian,' said Robin.

'Don't worry, the forest will be our home dear Robin!'

'Let's get married on the same day Robin,' interrupted Will. 'Not to each other of course!' he added smiling.

1. **rushed:** 倉促 ▶SYN◀ to hurry
2. **proud:** 感到自豪
3. **blessing:** 祝福 ▶SYN◀ consent

'What a wonderful idea!' exclaimed the girls.

'Why don't we get married today?' suggested Will.

'I am sorry my friend,' said Allan, 'but I must return immediately to Nottingham Castle to save my Christabel. Your wedding will have to wait a little longer, I'm afraid.'

'Well in that case,' said Robin, 'let's wait until we have solved Allan's problems. Then we can have a triple[1] ceremony!'

They all thought this was a good idea, so Robin and Allan left for Nottingham Castle that same day.

A few days later, a pale-faced[2] Christabel stood looking at herself in the mirror. She was wearing a beautiful white dress which was in stark[3] contrast with the sadness in her eyes.

Just then Sir Tristan entered the room:

'My dear, I cannot begin to describe how beautiful you are!' he exclaimed. 'Come! It is time to go to Linton Abbey, where they are waiting to start our wedding ceremony.'

'Please Sir, listen to me,' begged[4] Christabel. 'I do not love you. My father has given you false

1. **triple:** 三重的 ▶SYN◀ for three
2. **pale-faced:** 面容蒼白的
3. **stark:** 顯然易見的 ▶SYN◀ very evident
4. **begged:** 乞求 ▶SYN◀ to implore

hopes. I cannot make you happy!'

Sir Tristan had no intention of losing his bride.

'Do not worry, you will learn to make me happy,' he replied and led the heartbroken[1] girl out of the room.

At Linton Abbey, everything was ready for the wedding ceremony. The bishop[2] was there with some monks and the church was full of flowers.

While they were waiting for the couple to arrive, a man appeared with a harp[3].

'Is there a wedding here today?' the stranger asked the bishop.

'Yes, but why do you ask? Are you a musician?'

'The best harpist in the country!' replied the stranger. 'May I play for the happy couple?'

'Yes, why not!' said the bishop. They all stood at the church door, and as the couple were about to enter the church, Christabel turned to her father and said:

'Please, father, if you have any love for your only daughter, then stop this madness[4] now!'

'Silence!' was all her father had to say.

'Stop!' shouted a loud voice.

1. **heartbroken:** 心碎的
2. **bishop:** 主教
3. **harp:** 豎琴
4. **madness:** 瘋狂的行為

'Who was that?' asked the Sheriff.

The musician took off his cloak[1] and sounded his horn three times.

'Oh no, not Robin Hood again!' cried the Sheriff.

'Yes, with my Merry Men!' said Robin, pointing[2] to the group of men now surrounding[3] them.

Then an elegant knight appeared next to Christabel and taking her hand he said:

' My darling Christabel, will you marry me?'

'Oh Allan! Allan!' exclaimed Christabel, recognising him immediately. 'Yes, yes of course I will!'

The Sheriff was furious but could do nothing.

The bishop ran away, so the monk who had helped Robin save Will did the wedding ceremony.

Then the Gamwells arrived with Maude and Marian.

'Two more happy couples to be married!' shouted Little John, as William and Robin led their loved ones to the altar[4].

So that day, three happy couples left the church, while Sir Tristan and the Sheriff walked angrily back to the castle. ▪

1. **cloak:** 斗篷 ▶SYN◀ cape, mantle
2. **pointing:** 指着 ▶PET◀ ▶KET◀ ▶SYN◀ to indicate
3. **surrounding:** 包圍 ▶PET◀ ▶SYN◀ to encircle
4. **altar:** 聖壇

PET-Reading

1 Read the following summary and choose the correct word for each space from A, B, C or D.

Next morning the Sheriff _____ *c* _____ up in a terrible mood.
A waked up **B** has woken up **C** woke up **D** wakes up

The Sheriff of Nottingham decided to make the local people pay (1)_____ tax. He hoped Allan Clare had (2)_____ in the forest. He wanted Christabel to get married (3)_____ Sir Tristan. Sir Tristan wanted the ceremony in Linton Abbey (4)_____ of the Castle Chapel. The Sheriff thought that if the wedding (5)_____ in the Castle, it would be (6)_____ for Sir Tristan. Will Scarlett couldn't marry Maude immediately because Allan hadn't solved his problems (7)_____. At the Abbey, thanks to Robin and his Men, Christabel was reunited with Allan. The Gamwells arrived with Maude and Marian, so the three young couples were (8)_____ to get married at last.

1	**A** much	**B** more	**C** many	**D** very
2	**A** dead	**B** died	**C** dying	**D** dies
3	**A** with	**B** at	**C** from	**D** to
4	**A** rather	**B** contrary	**C** instead	**D** near
5	**A** has been	**B** is	**C** were	**D** will be
6	**A** safer	**B** safety	**C** more safe	**D** most safe
7	**A** already	**B** still	**C** yet	**D** just
8	**A** could	**B** can	**C** ought	**D** able

Vocabulary

2 Match the following words to their correct definition.

z	Mood	**z**	your state of mind
1	widow	**a**	A container where you can keep treasure.
2	wedding	**b**	A woman whose husband has died.
3	murderer	**c**	A stringed musical instrument.
4	chest	**d**	A person who commits a crime by killing someone.
5	harp	**e**	The main part of a church.
6	altar	**f**	Marriage ceremony.

Writing

3 You are Sir Tristan and you want to invite your friend to your wedding. In your note you should:
- invite your friend to the ceremony
- tell him where and when the wedding will be
- explain how to get there

Write **35-45 words.**

Before-reading Activity

Speaking

4 The title of the next chapter is 'A Poor Knight and a Rich Bishop'. Discuss the following questions with your partner. Then read and check your answers.

1 Why do you think the Knight is described as 'poor'?
2 How will Robin help the Knight?
3 Where will the Rich Bishop meet Robin Hood?
4 What will happen to the Rich Bishop?

Chapter 5

A Poor Knight and a Rich Bishop

▶ 6 Marian lived happily in Sherwood Forest with Robin and his Merry Men.

Robin taught her to use a bow and arrow and she soon became quite expert.

Marian was queen of the merry group. Robin treated his men with kindness and considered them friends, so they all respected his authority.

Meanwhile, the bishop and the Sheriff of Nottingham went to the King. They told him that Robin Hood was a dangerous outlaw. The King ordered his men to catch Robin and kill him.

The King also raised[1] taxes again. This made life more and more difficult for the poor ordinary people of Nottingham. Robin Hood and his men continued to give them all the money they stole from the rich visitors to Sherwood Forest.

One day Robin, Will Scarlett and Little John stopped to rest under a big tree. This was their usual meeting

---

1. **raised:** 增加 ▶PET◀ ▶SYN◀ to increase

place. It was a warm spring day and everything was calm. The three men suddenly heard the noise of a horse not far away[1].

'Ah maybe this is our chance to help some rich nobleman lighten[2] his bags,' said Robin with a smile.

Little John stood up to see better and confirmed: 'Yes indeed, Robin. I can see a knight on horseback, but he looks very sad and his clothes are very old.'

'Probably he wants us to think he has no money,' said Will laughing.

'Yes I think you're right Will. Let's stop him and find out,' replied Robin, standing on the path[3] as the knight approached[4].

'Good afternoon stranger,' said Robin. 'Welcome to Sherwood Forest, we have been waiting for you'.

'Waiting for me?'

'Yes, my friend. I, Robin Hood always entertain[5] the people who pass through my inn.'

'Your inn?' repeated the stranger even more confused.

'Yes this forest is like an inn. I am your host and

---

1. not far away: 不遠 ▶SYN◀ near
2. lighten: 變輕
3. path: 小路 ▶PET◀ ▶KET◀
4. approached: 走近 ▶PET◀ ▶SYN◀ to come near
5. entertain: 招待 ▶PET◀ ▶SYN◀ to amuse

you are my guest[1]. Please come with me and we will eat and drink together.'

'Well in that case, I accept your invitation,' replied the hungry knight.

At their hideout, they prepared a big dinner for their guest with lots of meat and wine and the knight ate everything. At the end of the meal, Robin asked:

'Well my friend, have you enjoyed your meal?'

'Yes,' said the stranger.

'So now it's time for the bill[2]!' said Robin.

'The bill?' asked the knight, confused once more.

'Yes my friend. As I said, my forest is like an inn. You have eaten and now you must pay.'

'I'm afraid I only have two gold coins,' replied the knight sadly. 'I thought that you were a kind man Robin Hood and that you really wanted to help me.'

'I do not help those who can pay,' said Robin dryly[3], still convinced that the knight was a rich nobleman.

'But look at me!' exclaimed the knight. 'Can't you see that I am a poor man?'

'How can I believe you?' asked Robin. 'I often use disguise to fool[4] my enemies. Maybe you are

---

1. **guest:** 客人 ▶PET◀ ▶KET◀
2. **bill:** 賬單 ▶PET◀ ▶KET◀
3. **dryly:** 冷淡地 ▶SYN◀ abruptly, sarcastically
4. **to fool:** 愚弄 ▶SYN◀ to trick

doing the same to me. If you are telling the truth, then you will let my men look in your pockets.'

'No problem!' said the knight.

Robin waited while his men searched[1] the knight until Little John eventually said:

'See! This man has only two gold coins!'

Now Robin felt very embarrassed and apologising[2] to the knight, he said:

'I am so sorry. What is your name my friend?'

'Do not worry Robin Hood,' said the knight.

'My name is Sir Richard of the Plain and I was once a rich and carefree[3] man.'

'Please tell me your story and maybe I can help you,' said Robin.

'Well, my son Herbert is engaged[4] to a lovely girl called Lilias,' explained the knight. 'However, six months ago, an evil knight saw Lilias and fell in love with her. The next day, he abducted[5] Lilias while she was walking near our home.'

'Oh no!' exclaimed Robin and his men, who were sitting listening to the poor man's story.

'Herbert went to look for Lilias. When he found

1. **searched:** 搜查 ▶PET◀ ▶SYN◀ to examine, inspect
2. **apologising:** 道歉 ▶PET◀ ▶SYN◀ to say sorry
3. **carefree:** 無憂無慮的 ▶SYN◀ without worries
4. **engaged** 已訂婚的 ▶PET◀
5. **abducted** 誘拐 ▶SYN◀ to kidnap

her, there was a fight and he killed the knight,' continued Sir Richard.

'Then soldiers came and arrested Herbert, but I asked the King to have pity[1] on my son. He said he would pardon[2] Herbert if I paid him a large sum of money. I have sold everything but I still need 400 gold coins or my son will be hanged!' concluded the poor man crying.

When Robin heard these words, he whispered something to Little John. Little John disappeared, then quickly came back with a little leather pouch[3].

'Here my friend,' said Robin, giving the man the pouch. 'Take these coins and hurry to save your son, so that he can return to his loved one.'

The Knight was overjoyed when he saw that there were at least 500 pieces of gold in the bag.

'But how can I repay you?'

'Do not worry my friend,' answered Robin. 'I'm sure that another guest will soon pass this way!'

'Thank you my friend!' shouted Sir Richard as he rode away to pay off his debts[4] and save his son.

The next day, Robin sat down with his men to

1. **pity:** 憐憫 ▶PET◀ ▶KET◀ ▶SYN◀ compassion
2. **pardon:** 原諒；赦免 ▶SYN◀ to forgive, free
3. **pouch:** 小袋子
4. **debts:** 債務

talk. They were always happy to help people in need[1], but they did not have much money left now.

'I hope another guest visits us soon' said Will to Robin.

'Yes but this time a paying guest!' said Robin.

Just then, Much arrived.

'Robin!' he shouted, 'Guess who's coming to dinner?'

'Who?' asked Robin.

'The Bishop of Hereford!' exclaimed Much.

'This is what I call a lucky day,' shouted Robin. 'Quick men, let's go and give our guest a surprise welcome!'

They divided into three groups to cover all the forest. Robin and his group dressed up[2] as shepherds[3]. They sat in the middle of the path cooking a big piece of venison[4].

When the Bishop saw the shepherds, he stopped and got off his horse.

'What are you thieves doing with the King's deer?'

'We were hungry,' said Robin simply.

'What!' exclaimed the Bishop. 'Servants! I order you to capture these thieves!'

---

1. in need: 需要幫助的 ▶SYN◀ requiring help
2. dressed up: 假扮 ▶SYN◀ to disguise
3. shepherds: 牧羊人
4. venison: 鹿肉

But Robin sounded his horn, and soon his band of Merry Men arrived.

The Bishop recognised Robin and thought he was about to die. However, Robin said:

'Let's have dinner together at my camp!'

The Bishop was so surprised that he accepted immediately. When they reached the hideout, he saw the table full of food.

At first he only ate a little, but after lots of red wine, he soon relaxed and ate a huge[1] amount. All this time Robin chatted, and the Bishop thought he was very friendly.

'Well thank you, Robin Hood,' he said at last.

'Do not thank me, Sir,' replied Robin. 'Instead[2], I must thank you for what you are about to pay!'

'What do you mean, pay?' asked the Bishop.

'You have eaten, so you must pay,' said Robin.

He ordered his men to take all the Bishop's money. Then they put him, half-drunk[3] on his horse and sent him home.

'Good work!' said Robin to his men. 'Now we have money for the poor again!'

---

1. **huge:** 巨大的 ▶PET◀
2. **instead:** 反而 ▶PET◀ ▶KET◀ ▶SYN◀ on the contrary
3. **half-drunk:** 半醉的

Reading

1 **Match the characters to what they say. You can use the characters more than once.**

   a̲ 'Welcome to Sherwood Forest., we have been waiting for you.'

   1 ☐ 'I can see a Knight on horseback, but he looks very sad and his clothes are very old.'

   2 ☐ 'I am your host and you are my guest.'

   3 ☐ 'I'm afraid I only have two gold coins.'

   4 ☐ 'I was once a rich and carefree man.'

   5 ☐ 'I hope another guest visits us soon'

   6 ☐ 'Guess who's coming to dinner?'

   7 ☐ 'What are you thieves doing with the King's deer?'

a Robin Hood **b** Sir Richard of the Plain **c** Much
d The Bishop of Hereford **e** Little John **f** Will Scarlett

Vocabulary

2 **Complete the sentences with the words from the box.**

debts	~~horseback~~	coins	~~sad~~	truth
killed	pity	hungry	carefree	son

Sir Richard came towards Robin on _horseback_ and he looked very _sad_.

1 Sir Richard was very .... because he hadn't eaten for days.

2 He didn't have many gold ....

3 He was telling the .... when he said he was poor.

4 He was once a rich and .... man, but now he was sad and worried.

5 Sir Richard's .... Herbert .... the Knight who had taken Lilias away.

6 Sir Richard asked the King to have .... on his son.

7 Sir Richard paid off his .... with the money Robin gave him.

Grammar

3 **Put the verbs in brackets into the correct tense and complete each sentence with one of the expressions in the box.**

if	when	unless	as soon as	until	~~as long as~~

Robin's men will always respect him *as long as* he *treats* them with kindness.

1 .... the King's men .... (not catch) Robin Hood, the King will be very angry.

2 The King .... (not free) Herbert .... Sir Richard gives him lots of money.

3 Marian will live in the Forest with Robin .... he .... (get back) his home and land.

4 .... the Bishop visits the King next time, he .... (tell) him what happened.

5 Lilias and Herbert will get married .... they .... (can).

Before-reading Activity

Listening

▶ 7 **4** **Listen to the beginning of chapter 6 and complete the sentences with the words you hear.**

The King promised he would do everything to *catch* the outlaw.

1 He announced he would give a big .... to the man who captured Robin Hood.

2 He was a big .... man who didn't like working much.

3 He went from town to town looking for............................ .

4 He thought this was his .... to make some money.

Chapter 6

Jasper the Tinker

▶ 7   After his unfortunate adventure, the Bishop of Hereford went to see the King. The King promised he would give a big reward[1] to the man who captured Robin Hood.

Bamborough was a small town near Nottingham. A tinker[2] called Jasper lived there with his family. He was a big lazy man who didn't like working. He went from town to town looking for jobs, but was often found asleep under a tree.

Jasper heard about the reward offered by the King, and saw this as his chance to make some money.

'Wife,' he said one morning. 'Do not worry, if I am away for a few days, I am going to make my fortune!'

'Jasper, please, not another foolish[3] idea!'

'Just wait and see!' he said and ran out of the house before she could stop him.

First he got a special warrant[4] signed by the King. With this, he could arrest Robin Hood. Then he set out for Nottingham Forest.

---

1. **reward:** 獎賞 ▶PET◀ ▶SYN◀ prize
2. **tinker:** 補鍋匠
3. **foolish:** 愚蠢的 ▶SYN◀ silly, stupid
4. **warrant:** 令狀

Next morning Robin was going to Allan and Christabel's house, when he saw a tall, fat man on the road to Nottingham. He seemed happy.

'Good morning,' said Robin. 'What brings you to this part of the country?'

'I am looking for a robber[1] called Robin Hood,' said Jasper.

Robin looked at the man in surprise and asked: 'Why are you looking for him?'

'The King has promised to give a hundred gold crowns[2] to the man who captures the outlaw!'

'And how do you think you are going to capture him?' asked Robin, enjoying this conversation.

'Well I have an order[3] for his arrest in my pocket.'

'And do you think that with this piece of paper you'll manage[4] to catch the thief?'

'Do not worry stranger,' replied Jasper proudly. 'It won't be difficult for me, I am tall, strong and courageous!'

'Well, I'm glad to hear that,' replied Robin with a smile. 'And tell me, would you know this outlaw if you met him?'

1. **robber:** 強盜
2. **crowns:** 古時一種硬幣（相當於25便士）
3. **order:** 令狀 ▶PET◀ ▶KET◀
4. **manage:** 設法做某事 ▶PET◀ ▶SYN◀ to succeed

'No, I have never seen him,' said Jasper. 'If I knew what he looked like[1] it would be easier.'

'I've heard he's very handsome[2],' said Robin, trying not to laugh.

'Do you know him?' asked Jasper hopefully.

'Well actually, I have met him twice,' answered Robin. 'Maybe I could help you catch him.'

'I will share[3] the reward with you if you help me find this outlaw!' exclaimed the tinker.

'Good then!' said Robin, 'I'm always looking for ways to earn some money.'

'Listen,' he continued, 'yesterday someone told me Robin Hood will be in Nottingham today. If you come with me, I'll show you this famous outlaw if you want.'

'I cannot think of a better plan! Thank you my friend. You won't regret[4] helping me.'

'You can be sure about that!' said Robin.

So the two new 'friends' set off together. After four hours, they arrived just outside the town.

'Why don't we stop at this inn and have something to eat?' Robin suggested.

1. **looked like:** 看上去像 ▶PET◀
2. **handsome:** 英俊的 ▶PET◀ ▶SYN◀ good-looking
3. **share:** 分享 ▶PET◀ ▶KET◀ ▶SYN◀ to divide
4. **regret:** 後悔 ▶PET◀

'Good idea!' agreed Jasper.

Robin, knew the innkeeper[1] well and ordered a bottle of very strong beer. The tinker was very thirsty and drank all of it.

Then Robin asked for a bottle of wine. He took a little, then gave the bottle to Jasper who finished it. The tinker was now very merry[2] and said:

'Innkeeper, bring some more of your excellent beer and wine. My friend and I must celebrate because we are going to become rich very soon!'

The innkeeper looked at Robin and smiled. Then he followed the tinker's orders and brought more wine and beer.

While the tinker got drunker and drunker, Robin sat with the same glass of wine, waiting for the man to fall asleep. To pass the time, he asked him what he would do with his fortune.

'Ah my friend,' slurred[3] the tinker. 'That is a good question. First I will leave my wife who is always moaning[4] at me to find a job. Then I will spend all the money on good food and drink and I will never work again!'

1. **innkeeper:** 客棧老闆
2. **merry:** 微醉的
3. **slurred:** 口齒不清地說話
4. **moaning:** 埋怨 ▶SYN◀ to complain

'I am pleased to hear you have such noble intentions,' commented Robin dryly. The tinker was so drunk, that he didn't even notice Robin's sarcasm.

Jasper boasted[1] about how he would catch Robin Hood and all his band of Merry Men. The King would be so pleased that he would make him a knight. As he was speaking, he slowly fell off his chair onto the floor, where he lay fast asleep[2].

Robin immediately looked in the tinker's pockets. He found some money and the warrant for his arrest. Then, satisfied with his work, he paid the innkeeper saying:

'Thank you for your help, my friend. Here is the money for what we have drunk. However, when this foolish man wakes up, tell him he must pay you.'

'But Robin, what will I say if he asks about you?' asked the innkeeper.

'Tell him I am Robin Hood and that if he wants to speak to me, he can find me in Sherwood Forest,' said Robin laughing. With these words he went away, leaving the tinker sleeping under the table.

Much later, Jasper the tinker woke up with a

1. **boasted:** 吹牛
2. **fast asleep:** 熟睡的

very bad headache[1]. He slowly sat up and looked around him, trying to remember where he was.

A terrible thought came into his head. He put his hand in his right pocket, It was empty[2]! The warrant was gone! That wicked man had stolen his chance[3] of happiness!

Then he felt in his other pocket where he usually kept his money. Gone! Everything was gone!

'Innkeeper! Innkeeper!' shouted the tinker. 'Help me, I have been robbed!'

The innkeeper looked up and said calmly: 'Who has robbed you?'

'That man I was drinking with!' shouted the tinker. 'He has stolen all my money!'

The innkeeper now pretended[4] to be angry.

'Well that's great! Now who is going to pay me?'

'What!? Do you mean I have to pay the bill?'

'Well, you're the one who drank the most!'

''I'm sorry, but I have nothing left. I had an order to arrest Robin Hood. I was going to make my fortune,' said the tinker.

'That man promised to help me! How stupid I

1. **headache:** 頭痛 ▶PET◀ ▶KET◀
2. **empty:** 空的 ▶PET◀ ▶KET◀
3. **chance:** 機會 ▶PET◀ ▶SYN◀ opportunity
4. **pretended:** 假裝

have been!' wailed[1] the tinker.

'Well yes,' agreed[2] the innkeeper, 'but if you say you came here to capture Robin Hood, then why were you drinking with him?'

The tinker looked at him in horror.

'What?' he exploded, 'What do you mean?'

'I mean you have just missed your chance of capturing Robin Hood.'

'But how? When? Where?' asked the tinker.

'My foolish traveller,' said the innkeeper. 'Robin Hood left while you were sleeping. You arrived together and drank together, I thought you were one of his Merry Men.'

The tinker sat down and put his head in his hands. 'I must find him,' he said.

'Well, he'll be somewhere in Sherwood Forest, but before you go, you must pay the bill.'

'I have no money left. All I have is my tools[3]!'

'Then go with your tools and find an honest job!' said the innkeeper, pushing him out the door. Jasper walked home sadly and wondered what he would say to his wife this time.

---

1. wailed 哀號 ▶SYN◀ to cry
2. agreed 同意 ▶PET◀ ▶KET◀
3. tools 工具

After-reading Activities

Reading

1 Decide if the following sentences about Jasper the Tinker are true (T) or false (F).

	T	F
He was a hard-working man.	☐	☑
1 He travelled about looking for work.	☐	☐
2 He wanted to catch Robin Hood.	☐	☐
3 Jasper was tall and slim.	☐	☐
4 He didn't recognise Robin Hood when he met him.	☐	☐
5 He didn't drink much at the inn.	☐	☐
6 Robin stole Jasper's money.	☐	☐
7 The innkeeper took Jasper's tools.	☐	☐

Grammar

2 Robin goes back to his hideout and that evening he tells his men what happened that day with Jasper the Tinker. Complete his story with the verbs in the Simple Past or Past Continuous.

'Well this morning (0) *I was going* (go) to Allan and Christabel's house, when (1) I _____ (meet) a stranger on the road to Nottingham. He said his name (2) _____ (be) Jasper and that (3) he _____ (look for) a robber called Robin Hood!

(4) I _____ (think) this was really funny but (5) I _____ (not say) anything. Instead, (6) I _____ (tell) him that (7) I _____ (know) Robin Hood well and that I would be happy to help him. So, (8) we _____ (walk) together for four hours and when (9) we _____ (be) near the town, (10) I _____ (suggest) stopping for something to drink at the inn. Well, Jasper (11)_____(be) very thirsty and he soon (12) _____(get) very drunk. Finally (13) he _____ (fall) asleep and (14) I _____ (take) his money and the warrant for my arrest from his pockets and (15) _____ (leave) him sleeping in the inn!

66

Vocabulary

3 **Find these words in the wordsearch.**

adventure ~~tinker~~ reward warrant foolish merry

drunk headache chance

T	R	F	E	I	D	P	S	K	L
I	F	O	O	L	I	S	H	R	B
N	C	F	R	W	M	W	H	C	M
K	W	H	E	A	D	A	C	H	E
E	A	T	R	W	F	R	D	A	R
R	E	W	A	R	D	R	H	N	R
A	T	R	C	H	R	A	D	C	Y
D	I	E	H	A	U	N	R	E	C
F	A	D	V	E	N	T	U	R	E
A	X	I	L	J	K	B	R	A	H

4 **Match the words from exercise 3 with their definitions.**

A person who repairs pots and pans
made of tin.   *tinker*
_____

1 Written permission to arrest
somebody.   _____

2 Money which you are given as
a prize for doing something.   _____

3 Silly, stupid.   _____

4 Very happy.   _____

5 A pain in your head.   _____

6 An opportunity.   _____

7 An exciting or strange experience.   _____

8 How you feel after too much beer
or wine or other alcoholic drinks.   _____

Chapter 7

Sir Guy of Gisborne

▶ 8　It was spring. Robin and some of his men had moved to Barnsdale Forest to look for deer. On hearing this, The Sheriff of Nottingham decided to attack the rest of the Merry Men in Sherwood Forest.

However, the people of Nottingham, were grateful[1] to Robin and his men for all their help over the years. They told Robin's men about the Sheriff's plan. When the Sheriff and his soldiers arrived, the Merry Men were ready to fight. Once again, the Sheriff had to run back to the safety of his Castle.

The next day Sir Guy of Gisborne came to Nottingham Castle, and the Sheriff told his friend about Robin Hood and what had happened.

Sir Guy was an evil, arrogant man. He was cruel and bloodthirsty[2] and committed a lot of unjust deeds[3].

'I fear no-one my dear friend,' said Sir Guy. 'I would be happy to kill this stupid outlaw for you.'

'I must warn[4] you Sir Guy that this villain Robin Hood is very clever and I think it would

1. **grateful:** 感激的 ▶PET◀ ▶SYN◀ thankful
2. **bloodthirsty:** 殘暴的 ▶SYN◀ sanguinary
3. **deeds:** 勾當 ▶SYN◀ action
4. **warn:** 警告 ▶PET◀

68

be difficult even for you to catch him.'

'Do not worry, I am younger and stronger than you,' replied Sir Guy. 'Tell me where he is, and I will find him and kill him for you.'

'Well in that case, let's go together to Barnsdale Forest to capture the villain[1]!' shouted the Sheriff. So they set off with their soldiers.

Sir Guy was not only wicked but also clever. He decided to disguise himself as a hunter[2] so he could look for Robin Hood in the forest, without being disturbed.

He told the Sheriff and his soldiers to wait for him in another part of the forest until they heard his signal.

'When you hear my horn, you will know that I have cut off Robin Hood's head!' he said with an evil smile.

'Then I will wait impatiently to hear that sound!' replied the Sheriff of Nottingham.

Leaving the Sheriff and his men, Sir Guy went in the opposite direction. He hoped to come face to face with his victim.

He didn't have long to wait, because some villagers had warned Robin that the Sheriff was approaching Barnsdale.

1. **villain:** 壞蛋 ▶SYN◀ bandit
2. **hunter:** 獵人

Robin's men were hiding in different parts of the forest, so he was alone when Sir Guy appeared. Robin looked at this strange hunter from behind a tree. There was something odd[1] about him. The man had a big sword and looked evil. He decided to find out why he was there.

Meanwhile, Little John found the Sheriff and some of his soldiers sitting under a tree. He decided to attack them since there were only a few of them. This big giant however, was not as clever as Robin, and the soldiers caught him easily and tied[2] him to a tree.

'I will not kill you until you have seen your leader's head on the end of Sir Guy of Gisborne's sword!' laughed the Sheriff.

Little John was afraid when he heard Sir Guy's name. This man was well-known for his skill[3] and his cruelty so he was worried about his friend Robin. Why had he been so stupid? Now he could not help his friend.

On the other side of the forest, Robin appeared in front of the stranger and said:

1. **odd:** 古怪的 ▶SYN◀ strange
2. **tied:** 綁 ▶PET◀ ▶SYN◀ to bind
3. **skill:** 技巧 ▶PET◀ ▶SYN◀ ability

'You seem a brave and honest man, can I help you?'

Sir Guy looked at this young man dressed in green, but wasn't sure if he was Robin Hood.

'I am lost,' replied Sir Guy.

'Tell me where you want to go,' replied Robin. 'I know these paths very well.'

'To be honest, I want to go to the centre of the forest to catch a villain,' said Sir Guy.

Robin was surprised by these words but showed[1] no emotion.

'And who is this villain?'

'His name is Robin Hood and I will be happy to cut off his head for my friend the Sheriff!' exclaimed Sir Guy.

Again Robin controlled his emotions, but he slowly moved his hand nearer his sword.

'That seems a strange way to have fun[2],' said Robin dryly. 'And tell me, what is your name?'

'I am Sir Guy of Gisborne and you?'

'The man you are looking for, Robin Hood at your service!'

---

1. showed: 顯示 ▶PET◀ ▶KET◀ ▶SYN◀ to reveal, demonstrate
2. to have fun: 作樂 ▶SYN◀ to enjoy oneself

Both men immediately drew[1] their swords and started to fight.

Robin fought hard, but fell and suddenly Sir Guy's sword was at his throat.

'Prepare to die! Then I will sound my horn to tell the Sheriff that I have your head on my sword!' said Sir Guy.

Just then, a bird flew at Sir Guy's face and startled[2] him. Robin had just enough time to jump to his feet again.

Before Sir Guy could react, Robin plunged[3] his sword into the wicked man's chest, killing him instantly.

Robin sat on the ground exhausted. He silently thanked the little bird that had saved his life.

Then he cut off his enemy's head with Sir Guy's own sword. He put on the dead man's clothes, and sounded Sir Guy's horn.

Not far away, he heard shouts of joy. The Sheriff and his soldiers thought Sir Guy had won the fight. Robin went in the direction of their cries.

When the Sheriff saw a man approaching with

1. **drew:** 拔出
2. **startled:** 嚇一跳 ▶SYN◀ to surprise
3. **plunged:** 插入

a head on his sword, he was overjoyed. He was sure it was Sir Guy who had won.

Robin was very good at disguising himself and even walked like Sir Guy. He also made sure the head on the sword was facing him. Suddenly he saw Little John tied to the tree. Quickly, he thought of a plan to free his friend.

He walked towards[1] Little John and said:

'Since I have killed Robin Hood, as my prize, I ask you to give me this villain too. I wish to add his head to my collection!'

'Of course, of course!' exclaimed the Sheriff.

Only Little John recognised his master's voice. Robin came close[2] to him and untied[3] his hands and feet.

Then, Robin pulled the head off the sword and threw it at the Sheriff. Little John grabbed[4] the sword and used it to defend himself, while Robin sounded his horn. Soon, the rest of his men arrived to help them.

The Sheriff looked at the scene in disbelief and could only do as he always did. He ran off like a coward, quickly followed by his soldiers. ▪

1. **towards** 朝着
2. **close** 接近 ▶PET◀ ▶KET◀ ▶SYN◀ near
3. **untied** 鬆綁 ▶SYN◀ to free
4. **grabbed** 緊握 ▶PET◀

After-reading Activities

Grammar

1 **Choose the correct alternative.**

The Sheriff of Nottingham decided *attacking / to attack* the rest of the Merry Men.

1 The people of Nottingham *was / were* grateful to Robin and his men for all their help.

2 The Sheriff *should / had to* run back to his castle because Robin's men were too strong for his soldiers.

3 Sir Guy disguised himself *as / like a* hunter.

4 He wanted to look for Robin without *be / being* disturbed.

5 Little John tried to attack the soldiers since there were only *a little / a few* of them.

6 Robin was *surprised / surprising* by Sir Guy's words.

7 Robin was very good *in disguising / at disguising* himself.

Writing

2 **Write a letter from Robin to Marian, telling her about what happened with Sir Guy of Gisborne.**
You should begin as follows. Write about 100 words.

Dear Marian,
Today a little bird saved my life!

▶ 9 **3** **Listen to chapter 8 and choose the correct answer - A, B or C.**

The Sheriff continued to live in Nottingham Castle
A ☐ with all his soldiers.
B ☐ with his daughter.
C ☑ by himself.

1 Christabel
A ☐ was happy when her father died.
B ☐ was not with her father when he died.
C ☐ still loved and respected her father.

2 King John
A ☐ was the same as his father King Henry.
B ☐ was better than his brother Prince Richard.
C ☐ was worse than the previous king.

3 King John
A ☐ loved the local people and was generous.
B ☐ did not like Robin because he was kind.
C ☐ loved passing through Sherwood Forest.

4 King John decided to spend some time in
A ☐ Sherwood Forest.
B ☐ Nottingham Castle.
C ☐ the Holy Land.

5 Richard was known as 'Richard the Lion Heart'
A ☐ because he hunted lions.
B ☐ because he was a courageous fighter.
C ☐ because he was holy.

6 When Richard came back to England
A ☐ he fought for many years.
B ☐ he thought England was a wealthy state.
C ☐ he was very sad about the conditions in England.

Chapter 8

King Richard the Lion Heart

▶ 9   After this last episode, the Sheriff spent the rest of his days in Nottingham castle alone. He was old and his soldiers had gone away. He died one winter night. His daughter Christabel was still happily married to Allan Clare. She was not with her father when he died. This saddened her, even if she had lost all love and respect for him a long time ago.

Three years passed, then King Henry died too, leaving the throne[1] to his sons. The poor people of England thought that at last, their lives might be easier, but they were wrong. Prince Richard, who was more honest than his younger brother John, decided to go and fight in the Holy Land[2]. So, Prince John became King. Henry had been bad, but John was even worse. The poor people suffered even more because of this weak, greedy ruler[3]. Crime grew[4] in the towns and the people had very little money to buy food.

Robin Hood and his Men continued to help the poor as much as they could, and local people

---

1. throne: 王位 ▶SYN◀ King's chair
2. Holy Land: 聖地（耶路撒冷及周邊地區）
3. ruler: 統治者 ▶SYN◀ soverign
4. grew: 增加 ▶PET◀ ▶KET◀ ▶SYN◀ to increase

loved them for their endless[1] generosity. Robin became famous all over England for his heroic deeds. The nobility and clergy[2] hated him because they had to pay whenever they passed through Sherwood Forest.

One summer, King John decided to go and stay in Nottingham Castle. The mad, selfish King decided to send his troops into Sherwood Forest to look for Robin Hood. He stayed in the safety of the castle while Robin's men easily defeated his soldiers.

Meanwhile in the Holy Land, Richard was now known as 'Richard the Lion Heart' for his bravery in battle. After many years of fighting, he decided to come back to England. He was horrified when he saw the terrible state[3] of England and his people.

He set off immediately for Nottingham Castle to arrest his brother John for treason[4] and reclaim[5] his title to the throne.

However, Richard's army was small and risked losing the battle.

Suddenly a group of men dressed in green came to the rescue. With a volley[6] of arrows, they helped

---

1. **endless:** 無盡的 ▶SYN◀ infinite
2. **clergy:** 神職人員
3. **state:** 情況 ▶SYN◀ condition
4. **treason:** 叛國 ▶SYN◀ betrayal
5. **reclaim:** 重奪 ▶SYN◀ to get back
6. **volley:** 群箭齊發

defeat the enemy. John was arrested and Richard was once more proclaimed King of England.

After celebrating his victory, the King asked his men about the brave archers. They had disappeared after the battle and he wanted to thank them for their help. So he sent some of his servants into town to question the local people.

'Your Majesty,' said one of his servants, 'the locals say that the leader of the men in green is called Robin Hood. He was once a nobleman with land but is now forced to live in the forest like an outlaw. They say he takes from the rich to give to the poor.'

'His intentions sound noble, not those of a common outlaw,' said the wise[1] King. 'How can I meet this man?'

'Well, apparently the only way to meet him is when he stops you, as you pass through his forest, to rob you.'

'Is that not a bit dangerous?' asked King Richard.

'No, Your Majesty, because Robin Hood is not a violent man and never harms his rich guests.'

---

1. **wise:** 有智慧的 ▶PET◀ ▶SYN◀ sensible, experienced

'His guests? What do you mean?'

'Robin invites the travellers to dinner, then makes them pay at the end.'

'This man is clever and has a good sense of humour too,' laughed King Richard. 'Tomorrow I will go to Sherwood Forest, dressed as a rich bishop and wait for Robin Hood!'

The next morning, the King was riding through the forest in disguise[1] with some servants, when Robin Hood appeared in front of him with his men.

'Good Morning,' said Robin pleasantly, 'I have been waiting for you. Breakfast is ready!'

King Richard immediately realised this man was Robin Hood, and wanted to smile.

Instead he said: 'How dare[2] you stop a Holy Man! Let me pass!'

'With the generosity of holy people like you, I can feed the poor,' replied Robin calmly.

King Richard was amazed by Robin's clever answer, knowing that all Bishops liked to be considered generous.

'Well, here are twenty gold coins,' he said.

1. in disguise: 偽裝
2. dare: 斗膽

'Your kindness astonishes[1] me!' said Robin, 'but let's eat before you must pay the final bill.'

At this point, the King laughed aloud, and it was Robin's turn[2] to be surprised. Then he took off his bishop's hat to reveal[3] his crown. Robin suddenly realised who he was talking to, and fell to his knees saying:

'My King and my Master, please forgive[4] me.'

Looking kindly at this brave young man, the King said:

'Robin Hood, please stand up. You have served my people well in my absence. I pardon you for any crimes you have been unjustly accused of. You are a free man, you and your band of Merry Men!'

The Merry Men shouted:

'Long live King Richard the Lion Heart!'

'Moreover Robin, I declare that your lands and title of Earl of Huntingdon are yours again. I wish you a long life to enjoy them,' said the King.

Robin said nothing, but with tears of joy in his eyes, he realised that all his dreams had come true at last.

1. **astonishes:** 使吃驚 ▶SYN◀ to surprise
2. **turn:** 輪到 ▶PET◀ ▶SYN◀ moment
3. **to reveal:** 展現；揭露 ▶SYN◀ to show, uncover
4. **forgive:** 原諒 ▶PET◀ ▶SYN◀ to pardon

After-reading Activities

Grammar

1 Transform the following sentences from active to passive.

Robin and his Men helped the poor as much as possible.
The poor were helped by Robin and his Men as much as possible.

1 The local people love Robin Hood.
Robin Hood ....

2 King John hadn't trained his soldiers well.
King John's soldiers ....

3 They defeated the enemy with a volley of arrows.
The enemy ....

4 Robin has never harmed his rich visitors to Sherwood Forest.
The rich visitors..

5 Robin Hood invited the King to have breakfast.
The King ....

6 Robin had never stopped King Richard before.
King Richard ....

7 The King will pardon Robin for his crimes.
Robin ....

Reading

2 Decide if the sentences are true (T) or false (F).

		T	F
	The Sheriff of Nottingham died one morning in Spring.	☐	☑
1	Christabel was no longer in love with Allan Clare.	☐	☐
2	King Henry died after the Sheriff of Nottingham.	☐	☐
3	Prince Richard was older than Prince John.	☐	☐
4	John was a generous king and everybody loved him.	☐	☐
5	Robin Hood and his Men helped King Richard's army.	☐	☐
6	King Richard took a Bishop with him to Sherwood Forest.	☐	☐
7	Robin's real title was Earl of Huntingdon.	☐	☐
8	At the end of the story Robin was so happy he shouted for joy.	☐	☐

84

Writing

3 Write the questions for the following answers.

What kind of father was the Sheriff of Nottingham?
He was a cruel father and did not show any love for his daughter.

1 Why..?
Because he wanted to go and fight in the Holy Land.

2 What..?
King John ordered his people to pay more taxes.

3 Where...?
King John's troops looked for Robin Hood in Sherwood Forest.

4 What..?
In the Holy Land Richard was known as 'Richard the Lion Heart'.

5 What..?
He arrested his brother for treason.

6 Who..?
Robin stole from the rich.

7 How long...?
Robin had been waiting for his guest all morning.

Vocabulary

4 Complete the sentences with a word in the box.

~~castle~~   respect   crown   treason   clergy

The Sheriff of Nottingham died alone in his *castle*

1 King John did not care about his country and was arrested for ....

2 Christabel did not love her father and had no .... for him.

3 When King Richard took off his Bishop's disguise, Robin saw his ....

4 The rich people in England at that time were the .... and the nobility.

85

Robin Hood, Legend or Reality?

The outlaw Robin Hood is one of the heroes of the English Middle Ages. No-one knows if he really existed or if he is just a legend. We first find stories of Robin Hood in 14th century English ballads, short narrative songs, which were very popular in the Middle Ages.

Robin Hood is the hero of about 40 ballads, which describe his generosity to the poor and his kindness to women and children. Each ballad describes an episode in Robin's life, as he fights against injustice with his 'merry men'. In these ballads Robin is a rebel who steals from rich landowners or members of the Church.

Life in medieval England

The early ballads describe the cruelty which was part of everyday life in medieval England.

At that time in England, there were strict laws against hunting in the forest. It was also a period of great poverty among the country people of England, which led to the Peasant's Revolt in 1381. Therefore the poor people loved the legend of Robin Hood, the free outlaw, who hunted in the forest and fought against the authorities.

A changing story

Over the centuries, the stories of Robin Hood have been told time and time again. Each time some changes occur. In the early ballads, Robin Hood is a countryman. Then, during the 16th century, new ballads describe him as a nobleman who has lost his title and lands. Here he is known as Robert Earl of Huntingdon, born in Loxley. At this point they also concentrate more on the romantic aspects of our hero's life and Maid Marian is introduced into the story.

Historical Setting

One of the early ballads refers to King Edward. There were three kings called Edward between 1272 and 1377. However in the late 16th century, the story of Robin Hood is moved back in time until about 1190, when Richard 1st of England took part in the Crusades. Then in the 18th century, Robin Hood is transformed into a Saxon who fights against the noble Normans, and is mentioned in 'Ivanhoe' by Walter Scott.

David Bruce, King of Scotland, acknowledges Edward III as his feudal lord.

The Sheriff of Nottingham and Robin Hood

The Sheriff of Nottingham appears in the early ballads with Robin's other enemies, the rich clergy. However, he does not have a specific role. Then, in Alexandre Dumas' version called 'Robin Hood The Outlaw' it is the Sheriff of Nottingham who takes Robin's land from him. This is the version that we have followed in re-telling the story in this edition. His job is to stop people killing the King's deer in Sherwood Forest and to ensure the safety of the rich people who pass through the forest. However, he is a coward and not clever enough to outwit Robin Hood.

The Sheriff of Nottingham Today

This position actually still exists today, but in a totally different context. Nowadays, the Sheriff of Nottingham is no longer responsible for law and order. His job is to increase the number of visitors to Nottingham, mainly through the legend of Robin Hood. The Sheriff travels all over Britain and abroad to promote the city of Nottingham. So, even today Robin Hood indirectly continues to help the people of Nottingham by creating jobs for them in the tourist industry. However, this time he has a surprising ally, the Sheriff of Nottingham!

The Sheriff of Nottingham

Robin Hood in the 20th and 21st century

The story of Robin Hood has remained popular over the years and many films have been made about it. Each of them tells a different story, but Robin's courage and generosity are always present. Here we mention just some of the films based on the story of our legendary hero.

Cinema

One of the most expensive films of the 1920s was 'Douglas Fairbanks in Robin Hood'. It cost about 1 million dollars to make. In the Hollywood Studios, they constructed a setting which included a castle and a medieval village. Fairbanks wrote, produced and starred as Robin Hood in this version of the medieval legend.

In the 1973 Disney cartoon version, all the characters are animated animals. Each character is transformed into an animal which reflects his or her personality perfectly. Robin for instance is a fox, an animal famous for being a quick thinker, just like Robin. The Sheriff of Nottingham is a big grey wolf, an aggressive animal like the character of the Sheriff.

In 1991, Kevin Costner interprets the role of Robin Hood in the film 'Robin Hood: Prince of Thieves'. In this version, Robin returns to England after fighting in the Crusades. He joins a group of villagers in the forest to fight against the evil Sheriff of Nottingham.
In 2010, Ridley Scott's film 'Robin Hood' starring Russell Crowe, tells the story of our hero before he becomes an outlaw.
This time, Robin is a patriotic leader who fights with the English to defend their country against the French.

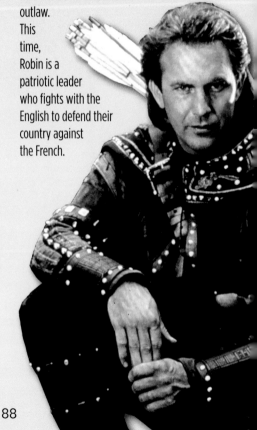

Television

The story of Robin Hood has also been adapted many times for television. ITV had a lot of success with their television series called 'The Adventures of Robin Hood'. It was really popular and was broadcast from 1955 to 1960 in the UK. Some of the episodes were based on the legend of Robin Hood, while others were invented by the writers of the series.

In 2006, the BBC broadcast another TV series called 'Robin Hood'. This programme was also very popular. Robin Hood was played by the actor Jonas Armstrong and the series followed the traditional stories of the legend. It ran for 3 years until the principal actor left the programme. It has been shown in many parts of the world.

1922: Swashbuckling US film actor Douglas Fairbanks (1883-1939), originally Douglas Elton Ullman plays British folk hero Robin Hood.

Kevin Costner interprets the role of Robin Hood in the film 'Robin Hood: Prince of Thieves', 1991.

Videogames

There are also a lot of video games on the market about Robin Hood.
These are usually strategy games involving clever tactics, which reflect the characteristics of the legendary figure. The player controls the movements of Robin Hood who must complete certain missions with his men. The missions differ according to each game. Many of these games also let the player decide how to end the story.

The East Midlands

The East Midlands is the name of the region in the central-east part of England and includes Nottinghamshire in its territory.

The word 'shire' means a division of land, and in the UK it is also another word for county. In the Anglo-Saxon period, royal officials called 'sheriffs', governed these shires. The sheriff had a lot of power and one of his main duties was to collect the taxes imposed by the King. Therefore he was not a popular figure among the ordinary people.

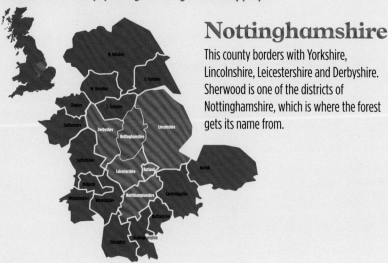

Nottinghamshire

This county borders with Yorkshire, Lincolnshire, Leicestershire and Derbyshire. Sherwood is one of the districts of Nottinghamshire, which is where the forest gets its name from.

The City of Nottingham

Apart from Robin Hood, Nottingham was also famous all over the world for its lace-making and bicycle production during the Industrial Revolution.

Nowadays, many big companies have their main offices in Nottingham. In the centre of the city there is the Old Market Square which is the biggest in the UK.

Nottingham Castle is to the west of the city. It looks over the city on a natural promontory called 'Castle Rock'. In the past, the Castle was very important for nobles and the royal family because it was near two important Royal forests, Barnsdale and Sherwood. It was a Royal residence until about 1600. Now special events connected to the legend of Robin Hood are held in the Castle every year, and attract many visitors from all over the world.

Barnsdale

In the original ballads, Robin's hiding place is Barnsdale Forest.

Barnsdale is in the county of Yorkshire, the biggest county in England, situated about 50 miles north of Sherwood. Barnsdale Forest now covers a small area of South Yorkshire. In medieval times it was a very big forest. This area was full of deer, and many royal hunts were organised there.

The people of Yorkshire are also proud of their connections with Robin Hood. In Barnsdale Forest there is '*Robin Hood's Well*'. They have also called the airport in South Yorkshire the 'Robin Hood Airport Doncaster Sheffield'.

Sherwood Forest

In the modern legends, Robin hides with his Men in Sherwood Forest. This forest still exists today, and can be found north of the city of Nottingham. In the past, it was a very big Royal hunting forest. Nowadays, it is a nature reserve and a big tourist attraction. Every summer, there is the Robin Hood Festival which lasts a week. They create a medieval atmosphere, and visitors can see many of the famous characters from the Robin Hood legends.

In some parts of the forest, there are still some very old oak trees. The oldest is the '*Major Oak*' and many people believe that this was Robin Hood's favourite hiding place.

Robin Hood's Well.

Oak tree in Sherwood forest.

Decide if the sentences are true (T) or false (F).

		T	F
	Yorkshire is in the East Midlands.	☐	☑
1	Sherwood is in the East Midlands.	☐	☐
2	Big companies in Nottingham produce bikes nowadays.	☐	☐
3	Members of the Royal family used to hunt deer in Sherwood Forest.	☐	☐
4	Nottingham Castle holds yearly events to celebrate the memory of Robin Hood.	☐	☐
5	The city of Nottingham has become an important business centre.	☐	☐

91

Test Yourself 自測

Choose A, B or C to complete the sentences.

At the start of the story the King on the throne is
A ☐ John   B ☑ Henry   C ☐ Richard

1 William Gamwell was known as Will Scarlett because of
A ☐ the colour of his jacket   B ☐ his red nose
C ☐ the colour of his hair

2 Allan Clare was
A ☐ Robin's cousin   B ☐ Maude's husband
C ☐ Marian's brother

3 To save Will, Robin dressed up as a
A ☐ monk   B ☐ shepherd
C ☐ musician

4 Allan Clare was rescued by
A ☐ Robin Hood   B ☐ Little John   C ☐ Much

5 Sir Tristan wanted to get married in
A ☐ Nottingham Market Square
B ☐ Linton Abbey
C ☐ Nottingham Castle Chapel

6 For his son's pardon, Sir Richard of the Plain still had
to pay the King
A ☐ 500 gold coins   B ☐ 400 gold coins
C ☐ 200 gold coins

7 When the Bishop of Hereford arrived, Robin Hood and
his Men were eating
A ☐ lamb   B ☐ beef   C ☐ venison

8 Jasper the tinker fell asleep in the inn because he was
A ☐ tired   B ☐ hungry   C ☐ drunk

9 During their fight Robin Hood and Sir Guy of Gisborne
each had a
A ☐ sword   B ☐ bow and arrow   C ☐ gun

10 King Richard the Lion Heart went to Nottingham Castle to
A ☐ embrace his brother John
B ☐ apologise to his brother John
C ☐ arrest his brother John

Syllabus 語法重點和學習主題

//

Topics
Love
Respect
Friendship
Loyalty
Courage
Generosity
Kindness

Grammar and Structures
Verb Tenses: present /past simple, present /past continuous, present / past perfect (continuous)
Question forms
Future tenses
Conditionals
Clauses with if, when, unless, as soon as , until, as long as
Modal verbs – present, past, future, conditional
Verb patterns
Synonyms
Adjectives, comparatives and superlatives
Adverbs
Prepositions
Too / enough
Direct / indirect speech
Active / passive

Functions
Express opinions
Make suppositions
Make requests
Make suggestions
Agree /disagree
Invite
Give information
Give directions
Apologise
Promise

Robin Hood

Pages 6-7

1 1 False **2** False **3** True **4** True **5** False **6** False **7** True
2a 1 d **2** a **3** e **4** c **5** b
2b 1 angry **2** help **3** rich **4** outlaw
3 **Across:** 1 Robin **4** just **6** leaf **7** let **8** team **9** rob **10** his **11** help **12** leader **13** archer
Down: 1 rich **2** Nottingham **3** deer **5** tree **10** hood **11** her

Pages 16-17

1 1 The Sheriff of Nottingham **2** King Henry **3** Will Scarlett **4** Robin Hood **5** Maude **6** Marian
2 1 is sitting **2** hasn't caught **3** met **4** had **5** aren't **6** hasn't seen **7** won't marry, has **8** blows
3 1 What colour of hair has Will Scarlett got? **2** Why does Robin steal from the rich? **3** Whose parents did the Sheriff of Nottingham kill? **4** When is Maude going to get married? **5** Whose brother is away fighting in the war? **6** How does Robin call his men? **7** What does an archer use to hunt deer? **8** How many men are there in Robin's band? **9** Whose name did Robin say while he was sleeping? **10** What happened on the day of the wedding?
(Answers to questions Ex 3 – done orally)
1 He has got red hair. **2** He steals from the rich to give to the poor. **3** He killed Robin's parents. **4** She is going to get married the following day. **5** Marian's brother is away fighting in the war. **6** He calls them with his horn. **7** He uses a bow and arrow. **8** There are about a hundred men in his band. **9** He said Marian's name. **10** Will Scarlett could not be found.
4 **Possible answers:** 1 Someone has taken him away. **2** He could be lost in the forest. **3** The man who looked at Will in the inn. **4** The man in the inn looked at Will in a strange way. **5** Send Robin's men into the forest and the town to look for him.

Pages 26-27

1 1 greedy **2** beautiful **3** ugly **4** rich **5** pretty **6** elegant **7** young
2

1 greedy	greedier	the greediest
2 beautiful	more beautiful	the most beautiful
3 ugly	uglier	the ugliest
4 rich	richer	the richest
5 pretty	prettier	the prettiest
6 elegant	more elegant	the most elegant
7 young	younger	the youngest

3 1 impatiently **2** immediately **3** well **4** sadly **5** triumphantly **6** instantly **7** quickly **8** angrily
4 1 no one as **2** young enough **3** to leave immediately **4** had taken **5** not to be

Pages 36-37

1 1 A **2** B **3** B **4** C **5** B **6** C
2 1 money **2** deer **3** thief **4** dungeons **5** gallows **6** sword
3 1 B **2** A **3** B **4** B **5** A **6** B **7** B

Pages 46-47

1 1 B **2** B **3** D **4** C **5** C **6** A **7** C **8** D
2 1 b **2** f **3** d **4** a **5** c **6** e

3 **writing sample answer:**
Dear George,
I would like to invite you to my wedding.
I'm getting married this Saturday at Linton Abbey.
Follow the road to Nottingham and turn left before you get to the castle. The abbey is there.
Regards
Sir Tristan

4 **speaking sample answers**
1 Maybe he has had bad luck or he has no money. **2** He will probably give him some money.
3 He might meet him in the forest. **4** Robin Hood will probably steal his money because
he is rich.

Page 56-57
1 **1** e **2** a **3** b **4** b **5** f **6** c **7** d
2 **1** hungry **2** coins **3** truth **4** carefree **5** son, killed **6** pity **7** debts
3 **1** if ... don't catch **2** won't free ... unless **3** until ... gets back **4** when ... will tell
5 as soon as ... can
4 **1** reward **2** lazy **3** jobs **4** chance

Pages 66-67
1 **1** True **2** True **3** False **4** True **5** False **6** True **7** False
2 **1** met **2** was **3** was looking for **4** thought **5** didn't say **6** told **7** knew **8** walked **9** were
10 suggested **11** was **12** got **13** fell **14** took **15** left
3

T	R	F	E	I	D	P	S	K	L
I	F	O	O	L	I	S	H	R	B
N	C	F	R	W	M	W	H	C	M
K	W	H	E	A	D	A	C	H	E
E	A	T	R	W	F	R	D	A	R
R	E	W	A	R	D	R	H	N	R
A	T	R	C	H	R	A	D	C	Y
D	I	E	H	A	U	N	R	E	C
F	A	D	V	E	N	T	U	R	E
A	X	I	L	J	K	B	R	A	H

4 **1** warrant **2** reward **3** foolish **4** merry **5** headache **6** chance **7** adventure **8** drunk

Pages 76-77
1 **1** were **2** had to **3** as **4** being **5** a few **6** surprised **7** at disguising
2 **Writing sample**
Dear Marian,
Today a little bird saved my life!
Today the Sheriff came with Sir Guy of Gisborne to look for me.
Sir Guy was dressed up as a hunter but as soon as I saw him, I thought there was something
strange about him. He was carrying a big sword.
Anyway I asked him if he needed any help.
He said he had come to the forest to catch a villain! Me of course!
Then he pulled out his sword and we started to fight. He was really strong and I suddenly foun
myself on the ground with his sword under my chin. I thought I was about to die, but luckily a
bird flew right into Sir Guy's face. I had time to jump up and took my chance and killed him.
See you soon,
Love
Robin

3 1 b 2 c 3 b 4 b 5 b 6 c

Page 84-85

1 1 Robin Hood is loved by the local people. 2 King John's soldiers hadn't been trained well. 3 The enemy was defeated with a volley of arrows. 4 The rich visitors to Sherwood Forest have never been harmed by Robin. 5 The King was invited by Robin to have breakfast. 6 King Richard had never been stopped by Robin before. 7 Robin will be pardoned by the King for his crimes.

2 1 False 2 True 3 True 4 False 5 True 6 False 7 True 8 False

3 1 Why did Prince Richard leave the throne to his younger brother? 2 What did King John do? 3 Where did King John's troops look for Robin Hood? 4 What was Richard known as in the Holy Land? 5 What did Richard do when he returned to England? 6 Who did Robin steal from? 7 How long had Robin been waiting for his guest?

4 1 treason 2 respect 3 crown 4 clergy

Page 91 CLIL

1 True **2** False **3** True **4** True **5** True

Page 92 Test yourself

1 c **2 c** **3** a **4** b **5** b **6** b **7** c **8** c **9** a **10** c